WAR SLUT

I0630244

CARLTON MELLICK III

ERASERHEAD PRESS
PORTLAND, OREGON

ERASERHEAD PRESS
205 NE BRYANT
PORTLAND, OR 97211

WWW.ERASERHEADPRESS.COM

ISBN: 1-933929-53-7

Copyright © 2006, 2011 by Carlton Mellick III

Cover art copyright © 2011 by Ed Mironiuk
www.edmironiuk.com

All rights reserved. No part of this book may be reproduced or
transmitted in any form or by any means, electronic or mechanical,
including photocopying, recording, or by any information storage
and retrieval system, without the written consent of the publisher,
except where permitted by law.

Printed in the USA.

Praise for
Carlton Mellick III

"Easily the craziest, weirdest, strangest, funniest, most obscene writer in America."
—*GOTHIC MAGAZINE*

"Carlton Mellick III has the craziest book titles... and the kinkiest fans!"
—CHRISTOPHER MOORE, author of *The Stupidest Angel*

"If you haven't read Mellick you're not nearly perverse enough for the twenty first century."
—JACK KETCHUM, author of *The Girl Next Door*

"Carlton Mellick III is one of bizarro fiction's most talented practitioners, a virtuoso of the surreal, science fictional tale."
—CORY DOCTOROW, author of *Little Brother*

"Bizarre, twisted, and emotionally raw—Carlton Mellick's fiction is the literary equivalent of putting your brain in a blender."
—BRIAN KEENE, author of *The Rising*

"Carlton Mellick III exemplifies the intelligence and wit that lurks between its lurid covers. In a genre where crude titles are an art in themselves, Mellick is a true artist."
—*THE GUARDIAN*

"Just as Pop had Andy Warhol and Dada Tristan Tzara, the bizarro movement has its very own P. T. Barnum-type practitioner. He's the mutton-chopped author of such books as *Electric Jesus Corpse* and *The Menstruating Mall*, the illustrator, editor, and instructor of all things bizarro, and his name is Carlton Mellick III."
—*DETAILS MAGAZINE*

Also by **Carlton Mellick III**

Satan Burger
Electric Jesus Corpse
Sunset With a Beard (stories)
Razor Wire Pubic Hair
Teeth and Tongue Landscape
The Steel Breakfast Era
The Baby Jesus Butt Plug
Fishy-fleshed
The Menstruating Mall
Ocean of Lard (with Kevin L. Donihe)
Punk Land
Sex and Death in Television Town
Sea of the Patchwork Cats
The Haunted Vagina
Cancer-cute (Avant Punk Army Exclusive)
War Slut
Sausagey Santa
Ugly Heaven
Adolf in Wonderland
Ultra Fuckers
Cybernetrix
The Egg Man
Apeshit
The Faggiest Vampire
The Cannibals of Candyland
Warrior Wolf Women of the Wasteland
The Kobold Wizard's Dildo of Enlightenment +2
Zombies and Shit
Crab Town
The Morbidly Obese Ninja
Barbarian Beast Bitches of the Badlands
Fantastic Orgy (stories)
I Knocked Up Satan's Daughter
Armadillo Fists
The Handsome Squirm

AUTHOR'S NOTE

Right now, I'm sitting in the Eraserhead Press office next to Cameron Pierce. I'm writing this introduction and he is doing final edits on a book he's releasing through Lazy Fascist Press called *Rico Slade Will Fucking Kill You* by Bradley Sands. About five days ago, I was behind the dumpster outside of a strip club, beating Cameron with a seven pound steelhead trout. He was wearing a muumuu and a granny wig. I was holding the big ass fish like a bat. When the cops were called they got a report of a transient being beaten with a fish by a gang of skinheads. Fellow bizarro authors Jeremy Robert Johnson and Jeff Burk were there, too. It was all Jeremy's idea. Jeremy is always the one who comes up with these kinds of ideas.

Let me explain. Cameron is getting married in a few days to new bizarro author Kirsten Alene. This was his bachelor party. Because Cameron is often referred to as a hobbit by his bizarro writer friends, mostly due to his small size and shire-esque hairstyle, his bachelor party wasn't just a big party full of whiskey and naked girls. It was a trial to prove whether or not Cameron was a hobbit or a man. On his quest, the hobbit was accompanied by an elf (Jeff Burk), an orc (me), and a wereman (Jeremy Robert Johnson). A wereman is a man who turns into a man on the night of a fullmoon, with a regular man's capabilities.

So Cameron had to do three stupid tests to prove he was a man, including dancing for dollars on a street corner, drive-by bowling, and getting beaten by a large fish. (Cameron is known for attacking people with fish, squid, and other meat products during his Meat Magic reading events. It was our time to get him back for that.) Once we found ourselves surrounded by four cop cars, Cameron didn't realize the cops weren't in on the joke and nearly got himself arrested for trying to fuck with them. All in all, it was a great night, but Cameron failed the last test by cheating, then he puked all over a bar, passed out, and we had to take him home early. So now Cameron will remain forever a hobbit.

What does any of this have to do with War Slut? Well, absolutely nothing. Except for maybe the fact that Cameron was the first person to ever buy a copy of this book, at a convention in San Francisco. He was just a fan then, an awkward teenager who came to the con with his grandma, but he would soon become one of the central figures in the bizarro fiction scene.

As an author, it's a really strange experience to realize that your work is actually affecting other people's lives. I don't write to affect anyone's life. I write for the fun of it. Whenever a reader tells me that my work has inspired them to become a writer, I don't know how to react to that. My first instinct is to tell them they need to find a better role model. My second instinct is to write some more books, because if this crap I write actually means something to somebody I've got a responsibility to write as much crap as humanly possible. It's good motivation.

So here is the re-release of my 15th book, War Slut. The book that pissed off most of my readers who serve in the military—not because it's an offensive statement against the United States military or the unending war in Iraq, but because the military elements in the story were poorly researched and completely unrealistic. They're right, of course, but it's still more realistic than G. I. Joe cartoons and those were all pretty awesome. So I'm okay with that.

—Carlton Mellick III   2/4/2011 9:31 pm

(Carlton Mellick III beating Cameron Pierce with a fish)

CHAPTER ONE
THE LOST BATTALION

The officers stopped talking this morning, stopped giving orders, so we're not quite sure what we should be doing.

We've been sitting here, in the snow-packed trenches, Corporal McClean going back and forth to the officers tent for an update but the officers won't even look at him, just sitting in director's chairs with cigars burning down to their knuckles, staring off into the frozen wasteland.

"Something's wrong," McClean says, pianoing his tattooed fingers at me.

That's all McClean ever says.

It's been five weeks since we arrived in the Arctic, five weeks of frostbite, five weeks of inane deaths. The war is over. It's been over for months. But we're still out here and nobody will tell us why.

On our way home, flying back to California, Colonel Dupont pointed his thin lightning bolt eyebrows at us and picked a scab off the wart on his thumb. He did this every time he had bad news for us.

"The war might be over for everyone else," he said. "But not for us."

There was another mission. One of utmost importance. He didn't give us any details. Didn't tell us the objective. Didn't tell us where we were headed. He just told us that the war wasn't over for us yet, and that we could take the stupid smiles off of our faces.

"There must still be some draft dodgers in hiding," the soldiers whispered to each other.

Draft dodger. The term makes my skin crawl. They are the final enemy of peace. The final enemy of freedom.

Every man, woman, and child in the world was drafted into the military to fight a war against the draft dodgers. This was years ago, long before I was born, long after all the nations of the world united as one. The cowards, rebels, traitors, anarchists. We thought we killed them all. But there were still a handful of them left. Somewhere.

"Any word yet?" LeForge asks the Corporal, sitting down next to me with frost on his glasses, adjusting the underwear in his pants.

McClean shakes his head and LeForge spits a glob of beef rations at him.

"It's not his fault," I tell LeForge.

"Bullshit," the large Frenchman says. "He's incompetent."

"He outranks you," I say.

LeForge flips me off.

McClean still has the beef goop on his chest, oblivious to the conversation, pianoing his fingers to some kind of tune in his head.

"So what the fuck are we supposed to do?" LeForge asks.

"Stand by," I say. "They'll give us orders when they're ready to."

A day passes. Still no orders.

Chauney comes out of a shelter with her grenade launcher flung over her shoulder like a backpack.

"Kot is dead," she says to me.

"That's all of them, then?" I ask.

She nods.

Only five of us left. Plus the officers.

We face each other for a while, crunching our feet in the snow.

"Maybe we'll be able to move on," I say, "now that the wounded have died."

She shrugs.

McClean tells the officers that Kot died during the night, but they still aren't listening to him. They haven't moved from their seats, smoking cigars and now sipping brandy, staring off into space without a care in the world.

"I'm like a ghost," McClean tells us.

LeForge kicks the snow.

"What are we supposed to do?" Chauney asks.

"What can we do?" I ask.

"We can do something," she says.

"What was their last order?" I ask.

"To bury Jefferson," Chauney says.

"Want to bury Kot?" I ask.

"Sure," Chauney says.

We bury Kot. It doesn't take very long.

"Now what?" LeForge asks.

"How about digging the rest of our graves, just in case?" Chauney says.

We shrug and dig the rest of our graves.

CHAPTER TWO
THE BATTLE WHORE

Another day passes.

The officers are done with their brandy. Their cigars have burned out against their fingers. Just sitting in their chairs, staring off into space.

I goop on another layer of climate camo. One of my last bottles. We're still dressed in desert fatigues, designed for the climate of North Africa where we had been stationed for the past three years. The only thing keeping us warm is the climate camo—a cream, thick as lipstick, that you spread on your entire body in harsh weather conditions that helps cool you in the heat or warm you in the cold. Unfortunately, it rubs off easily and there's not much of it left.

I'm happy Chauney is still alive. I haven't told her that I've fallen in love with her yet, but I hope to at some point soon, when the moment is right. It would have been horrible if she died with the others, before I told her how I felt about her.

She sits next to me, trying to warm her ammunition with her breath. Her thick black dreadlocks spill down from her head and flow over my lap. They must be three feet long. She's woven steel wool into the locks so they resemble chains more than hair.

They normally wouldn't let a soldier, man or woman, grow hair below the larnyx, but cutting hair goes against her religious beliefs so there's nothing any officer can do about it. All religious beliefs are protected by law.

I'm the only registered atheist I know. Most people choose a religion, whether they seriously believe in it or not, because religion has its benefits. You get holidays off with many religions. You get prayer breaks. You sometimes are allowed to receive presents from friends or family.

Chauney believes in a religion called Dookaduck. All of her superiors think she made up a new religion, which is against the law, but it is a true religion that is still practiced in Africa to this day. Since Chauney is of African descent, she is allowed to claim Dookaduck as her religion, even though she is only part African. Her father was a Scottish Italian and her mother was African Eskimo. But since her mother was three quarters African she was able to claim that she was mostly of African descent, and they granted her the right to believe in Dookaduck.

Unfortunately, the only benefit to this religion is that she gets to smoke a hallucinogenic herb once a year and grow dreadlocks as long as she wants.

Most of the other soldiers make fun of her hair. They tug on the locks when her back is turned or hide insects inside of them so that there'd be a special surprise for her later. But I've always thought her hair was beautiful and powerful. I was attracted to her the second I laid eyes on her.

"Have you seen Sweet lately?" Chauney asks me.

"No."

I realize that I have a hard-on, and that she's spotted it peaking out between her dreads in my lap. She laughs as I blush. I push her hair off of me and scuttle away.

"Where's Sweet?" I ask LeForge.

He's got oven mitts on his hands and is doing pushups in the snow.

"Freaking out again," LeForge says, counting his push-ups under his breath.

"Freaking out?" I ask.

"Keeps disobeying orders," he says. "Throwing tantrums."

"Whose orders? Yours?"

"Yeah," he says.

"You're at the bottom of the chain of command," I say. "You can't give orders to anyone."

"I can give orders to Sweet," he says. "Anybody can give orders to Sweet."

"Well, where is she?" I ask.

"He's somewhere. Hiding from me, I bet. They always hide from me."

"It's because you're an asshole," I tell him.

He flips me off while continuing to do push-ups one-handed.

I search all of the shelters, losing my hard-on as a breeze chills an inch of my neck where the climate camo has already rubbed off. It'll come back soon enough. All of the tents are empty, save one. McClean is sitting under a tarp made from a parachute, tattooing his ankle with a sewing needle.

"Seen Sweet?" I ask him.

He shakes his head.

McClean's uniform is always very neat. Not because he is very cleanly, but because he never actually does anything. He comes from a rich family where he never really had to do any work. The only reason he's been promoted to Corporal is because his dad is CEO of a popular sports shoe company.

Despite his last name, he's mostly of English descent. An English Protestant. Just like the Colonel. It's good to believe in the same religion as your superiors. They treat you like family. Being atheist, I was never treated well by many of my superiors.

"Crying Hugh Jake!" Sweet calls from one of the tents that had been empty just a few minutes ago.

"I've been looking for you," I say, entering the tent.

Sweet's standing there in the nude, penis swinging in the wind.

"How can you stand this cold?" I ask.

"The weather doesn't bother me. You know that."

I wipe the snow off of my ass and sit down on the sleeping bag. "Yeah, but that was Africa. It makes sense to walk around naked in that heat."

Sweet shrugs. "How's the Colonel?"

"Still ignoring us," I say.

"So we have free time?"

"I guess."

"So what do you want this time?"

"Chauney," I say.

"Again?" Sweet says. "You're so obsessed."

"I'm in love."

"It's going to drive you insane, you know that? You should just tell her how you feel."

"I know, I will," I say. "Eventually."

"Sure you don't want a nice Mexican girl?" Sweet asks.

"No. Chauney. Definitely Chauney."

"Whatever you want."

Sweet's body brightens into a yellow shine as bright as the sun. I cover my eyes. The glow mutates Sweet's body from a man into a woman.

The light fades and Sweet's body becomes Chauney, standing naked before me, smiling. She removes my wet clothing and crawls into a sleeping bag with me, wrapping her enormous dreadlocks around me like tentacles.

Sweet is the war slut—a genetically engineered soldier created to relieve sexual tension in combat situations. The war slut is able to change its gender and body shape to match the taste of the soldier it is servicing. Though I call her a she, Sweet is completely genderless. She's usually in the shape of a male during combat situations, but can take any shape she wants the rest of the time. As long as she doesn't impersonate an officer.

War sluts were brought into the military soon after the draft, when men first started fighting alongside women. There were several incidents of soldiers falling in love, incidents of rape, pregnancies, STDs, and a multitude of other problems. So the military started assigning prostitution duties to the more attractive male and female soldiers. They were ordered to sleep with any soldier in need of sexual relief, and were tested daily for diseases. This didn't completely solve the problem, however, because most of the war sluts resented their fornication duties. Many of them were driven to suicide.

The genetically engineered war sluts were developed a little later. They solved all these problems. Not only are they programmed to enjoy sex, but they also can change their shape into any dream lover a soldier can imagine. No need for condoms, the war sluts are self sterilizing against viral and bacterial infections. They also can't impregnate female soldiers or be impregnated by male soldiers. They are the perfect sex machine packaged within a perfect fighting machine.

I make love to Chauney.

She is the flavor of olives and raw hamburger meat. Her eyes are balls of orange and tan yarn. There is also a bit of pepper in there, but that is from Sweet. Sweet always has a peppery flavor no matter what shape she takes. My climate camo gets rubbed off of my chest as she fucks me; I can now feel the warmth of her breasts, her belly. She sucks the tongue out of my mouth and groans.

I cum inside of her and she lays her weight on top of me. She zips up the sleeping bag around us, stuffing her massive hair inside. It's like we're in a furry womb, holding each other, heating each other with our breaths.

I'm pretty sure Sweet is in love with me. If a war slut can feel love. We've been friends since Africa. I've been her only friend, because I'm the only person who treats her like a real human being. She's never made fun of my condition, or my tears. We've been a good team.

Sweet also likes that I call her a she, because her true form is a woman's. It's not really her true form. She's never had a true form, except maybe as a blob of flesh putty. But she says that she made up a form that she calls "the real me." It is how she sees herself on the inside, her soul in human form.

I'm the only person who knows about her true form. Others think of her true form as a large Latin soldier with a thin mustache. But I know that she is really a small mousy albino girl with silvery eyes and short curly hair. Once she asked if I'd like to have sex with her true form, as a joke.

We've been able to separate our sexual relationship with our friendship. It's easy for me to think of her as a different person when we screw, because she'll be in a different form. And when she becomes Chauney, I trick myself into believing she really is Chauney. Even with the peppery taste.

Though, thinking back, if Sweet really is in love with me it wouldn't have been easy for her to view me as somebody else when we made love. I might have viewed her as other people, but she just saw me, her best friend, every time. And maybe when she asked me to have sex with her true form she wasn't joking. Maybe she wanted to see if I would sleep with her, the real her. Maybe I hurt her feelings when I turned her down and asked her to transform into Chauney again.

Sweet used to tell me all of the other soldiers' dirty secrets. She told me their turn-ons, their fetishes, what types of people she transformed into for them.

She told me that the Colonel usually had her transform into a Catholic school girl from a picture he kept in his pocket. He normally didn't have sex with her in this form, but would masturbate onto her forehead or butt cheeks while she sucked on her thumb.

McClean was the most unusual. He had a very active imagination and always had her changing into the most outlandish women he could think of. At first he had her turning into simple playful fantasy women such as fairies or vampires or elves. Then they started getting less and less human: a devil girl with hot red skin, a mermaid, a medusa. Then he started getting into furries. He had her transform into bunny girls, cat girls, leopard girls. Then he got into plushies and she had to transform her skin to feel more like that of a fuzzy stuffed animal. Sometimes he would want her to have six breasts or extra arms. Sometimes he would want her to grow her clit to the size of a dick so she could fuck him in the ass. Sweet was very professional about it most of the time. She never turned him down once. But there was one time when she laughed in his face, and couldn't stop laughing until he ran out of her tent, when he asked if she could morph into the Japanese Anime character, Sailor Moon.

LeForge, however, was the worst. He didn't seem to enjoy sex. What he did enjoy was hurting people. The war slut was designed to take a lot of abuse from sadistic soldiers if that was their thing. They don't swell or bruise, but they can still feel pain. LeForge only had her transform into his enemies. Or anyone he was pissed off at. Sometimes it was the Colonel. Sometimes it was an ex-girlfriend who dumped him. Oftentimes it was McClean. He would order her to become whoever he was pissed off at that day, and then he would beat the living shit out of her and rape her until she bled. He couldn't cum until he saw blood, so he always brought a knife with him just in case. She used to cry after servicing LeForge. War sluts are supposed to be pretty dull to emotion, but LeForge made her cry. Especially on the days he had her turn into McClean and pretended to be raping him in the ass while punching him in the spine or kidneys, or rolling him onto his back so he could stare into his eyes as he strangled him and fucked him like a girl. Sweet refused him only once, when he wanted her to transform into me.

At that point, I should have known she had feelings for me. She was standing up for the man she loved. I could be wrong about all of this, but I'm sure she at least thinks of me as something a little more than a friend. I'm the closest thing she has to a friend, a family, a lover.

CHAPTER THREE
FINAL COMBAT

I didn't suspect Sweet had feelings for me until we were on the airplane leaving Kenya. She was in her true form through the entire flight, sitting next to me, not saying a word. And she was holding my hand. She looked devastated. Once the flight was over, she would never see me again. I would probably get stationed as a sales rep for a cell phone company and she would probably get assigned to a casino or an executive's lounge.

But I wasn't really worried about the end of my friendship with Sweet. I was more bothered by the fact that I probably would never see Chauney ever again. Before she came to Africa, she was stationed as a sawball player. Sawball is Chauney's obsession, and that's surely what she'll do once back in the states.

When Colonel Dupont told us that we weren't going home, Sweet almost seemed relieved and excited that we'd still be together for a short time. She held my hand even tighter. Her white curly fro resting against my arm. I didn't share her optimistic feelings of going back into combat. I was worried.

"Something's wrong," McClean said from the seat behind me.

I felt it too. There was just something unusual about all of this. The Colonel's lack of explanation. The tone of his voice. We were headed into a dangerous situation. And I was worried that we wouldn't make it through this one. Not myself, not Sweet, … not Chauney.

Chauney was the only thing I could think about as the plane went further and further north. Sweet was holding onto my side, but I hardly even noticed her.

Next thing we knew we were parachuting into a snow storm in the middle of the night onto blocks of ice somewhere in the Arctic Ocean. We were spread out pretty thin. Most of the soldiers landed in the water out in the dark. We could hear some of them calling out, lost in the freezing water, but Colonel Dupont didn't acknowledge them. He was in a hurry to move forward.

Sweet and I were lucky to be on one of the icebergs close to the Colonel. He was able to throw us a loose motor, even though there were only three of us on the block of ice. There was an iceberg with maybe a dozen soldiers to the west that just stood there, watching us as we put the motors in the water and propelled our ice block away from them.

Roaring through the Arctic waters on motorboats made of ice, we tried our best to keep up with the Colonel—who was all by himself on the smallest of the icebergs, which made him much faster than the rest of us.

He wasn't waiting up for anyone, zipping through the water as fast as he could, rubbing snow from his bald head and licking the wind out of his mustache. We were the second fastest and could hardly see him up ahead. The bulk of his troops were on one massive iceberg that was moving half the speed that we were, even though they had three motors propelling it.

McClean was also on the iceberg with us. He stood in the front, shining a spotlight so we could see through the storm. Sweet morphed into her Latin male form. She was at the motor, propelling us forward as water splashed against our faces like a shower of needles.

I was supposed to be Sweet's eyes and ears, but I was more concerned with losing Chauney. She made it safely onto one of the icebergs, but I was worried her group would get lost in the storm.

"Keep your eye on the Colonel," Sweet said every time I looked back to see if she was still behind us, even after we lost sight of him completely.

The water soon became slush and slowed us down. Then the slush became ice and we had to get off and continue on foot. Crackling noises under our feet with every step, but it supported our weight until we made it to thicker ground. Our supplies made us so heavy I'm surprised we didn't fall through.

"Is this land or just a bigger iceberg?" Sweet asked.

"We're in the Arctic," I told her. "There's only ice here."

We found the Colonel setting up camp half a mile in. He was pulling heavy machine guns out of waterproof crates and setting them up in a circle around the camp.

"Corporal," he said to McClean as if he had been by his side the whole time, "secure the perimeter."

McClean obeyed the order, armed himself with a slag-shot rifle, and rushed into the snow storm.

The Colonel ignored Sweet and I, as if we weren't even there. We stepped away from the camp and watched for the others. There were lights in the distance.

"Is it them?" asked Sweet.

I looked closer. There were a dozen and a half soldiers approaching.

I recognized LeForge right away. He was cleaning the snow off of his glasses and flexing his muscles at us. There was also Major Conifer and Lieutenant Chase. Then, holding up the rear, was Chauney.

Seeing her walking through the snow toward me put my mind at ease. Hair peppered with white flakes, grenade launcher draped over her shoulder, cool and calm as she's always been.

The Major and his men went straight for the heavy machine guns and fired a few rounds into the distance. Then they nodded at each other.

When Chauney arrived, I smiled and she half-smiled back. Sweet seemed almost angry that she survived, pinching her thin Latin mustache as hard as she could.

"How many made it?" Chauney asked me.

"Just us," I said.

"I guess there's more draft dodgers left," she said.

"Yeah," I said. "In the one place they thought we'd never look."

Then we went back to war.

CHAPTER FOUR
THE SILENT OFFICERS

Another day passes.

McClean refuses to go back into the officers tent, just shaking his head at us and hiding in his shelter. Chauney, LeForge, and I decide to check on them. They haven't moved in days. Just sitting in their chairs, staring into space.

"Sir?" I ask Major Conifer. "Is something wrong?"

No response.

"Can you hear me, sir?"

Nothing.

LeForge snaps his fingers in front of the Major's face. He doesn't even blink.

"Is he dead?" the Frenchman asks.

Chauney feels his wrist. "He's got a pulse."

We watch carefully. The Major licks his lips and sighs.

"Major?" Chauney asks.

No response.

It's like they just don't care to talk anymore, don't care to move, don't care to give orders.

"McClean was right," I say. "Something's wrong."

We try to feed the officers. They probably haven't eaten in days. They are dangerously dehydrated. I place a spoonful of green pea mush into the Colonel's mouth and lean his head back. Some of it slides down his throat but most of it foams out into his mustache when I open his mouth for the next bite.

McClean works on the Lieutenant, Chauney on the Major.

LeForge just gets in our way. He laughs at the officers and pokes at them and barks in their faces.

They don't try to stop him.

"It's like they're in comas," I say.

"No, they're not comatose," Chauney says. "They're consciously aware of everything happening around them."

"Even when I do this?" LeForge asks as he whips out his penis and slaps it against the Colonel's cheek.

"Yes," Chauney asks. "And once they're back to normal you're going to wish you hadn't done that."

"Not likely," LeForge says. "They're vegetables."

"I just told you they aren't comatose," she says. "They know exactly what is happening to them."

"Then why aren't they doing anything about it?" LeForge asks.

Chauney doesn't have an answer for him.

"They stopped talking because the war's over," McClean says, not making eye contact with any of us. "They had just won the final battle and realized the war is over. For good, this time. There will never be another war ever again. They are career officers, so they don't have anything else to live for anymore. They have no reason to talk, no reason to move. They've just given up on life."

It's the most I've ever heard McClean say.

"They just don't care anymore," he says.

We continue taking care of them for a few days.

A storm is coming in and the only climate camo we have left is what's already on our bodies. I cut up a parachute and sew it to my uniform for insulation. I've stopped carrying my gun around with me. Couldn't handle the cold metal. The food is running very low. LeForge thinks we can dig a hole in the ice and go fishing.

"Do you know how thick this ice is?" I ask him.

He just shrugs at me.

McClean continues tattooing himself.

"Come with me," Chauney says.

She brings me back to the officers tent, and puts her finger through a hole in the Colonel's back.

"What's that?" I say, bending in for a closer look.

A bullet hole.

"There's no blood," she says. "It must be some kind of chemical round."

"You think that's what did this to them?"

She nods. "All three of them have these wounds."

"None of the other soldiers in that battle had wounds like these," I say.

"I don't know," Chauney says. "Maybe they were just targeting the officers."

"You were there," I say. "Did you hear any slag-shots fired?"

"I didn't hear any before I was knocked out," she says. "We should talk to McClean ... or Sweet."

Sweet isn't in any of the tents. Probably hiding from Le-Forge again. And McClean is being sheepish about answering our questions.

"Did the enemy have slag-shots?" I ask.

McClean shrugs.

"Did you hear them or didn't you?"

"He wasn't even there," LeForge says. "He's a coward. He was probably hiding under the snow a mile away. We should hang him like a draft dodger."

"I was there," McClean says.

"And?"

"I don't know," he says. "I'm not sure if it really happened."

"What happened?" Chauney asks.

"It's not so easy to explain ..." he says.

Since we arrived in the Arctic, there has been only one battle. There have been reports of figures racing through the snowstorms, but nothing confirmed.

LeForge and I were left to guard the camp as everyone else went north. That was the last we saw of most of them. The story was that they were attacked on all sides, outnumbered by an enemy more experienced with the terrain. The Colonel, the Major, the Lieutenant, and McClean left the battle to get the wounded (Kot, Wilhelm, Jefferson, and Chauney) to safety. Nobody else survived. Except Sweet, who returned the next morning all by herself.

But McClean tells us something different ...

"We were all alone out there," he says. "I got a look at

Lt. Chase's wrist monitor. The only life signs on there were our own."

"Then what killed everyone out there?" LeForge asks.

"They killed each other," McClean says. "There's nobody out here. The officers have gone mad. They were chasing delusions, firing at ghosts until they got lost in the snow. They couldn't tell what was the enemy and started firing at each other. "

"They've lost it," he continues. "They didn't know what to do after the war ended so they brought us to the middle of nowhere to make up a new war."

He stops and we look at each other. We're not sure whether he's joking, crazy, or stupid. Or telling the truth.

"Find Sweet," I tell Chauney. "She was out there the longest."

LeForge: So we're out here for nothing?

McClean: We're all alone. Stranded.

LeForge: I bet nobody even knows we're out here!

Me: Stop it. We don't know what's going on yet. The officers all have slag-shots in them that aren't military issue. We think that's why they're catatonic.

McClean: They probably shot themselves.

Chauney returns.

Chauney: I can't find her.

LeForge: Who?

Chauney: Sweet, she's missing.

Me: Did you check everywhere? I'm sure she's hiding. She's been hiding a lot lately.

LeForge: Hiding from me, I bet.

Me: Yeah. Because you're such an asshole.

Chauney: No, she's not hiding. She's gone.

Me: Are you positive?

Chauney: She's left camp completely.

Me: McClean, you're in command now. What should we do?

LeForge: What!

Me: The officers are down. McClean is next in line. (To McClean) Are we going to go out there and search for Sweet or what?

LeForge: If McClean is in charge I'm going to mutiny.

McClean: Nobody is in charge! We're all going to die anyway. We can all die as equals.

Me: We need you. While you're still alive, you are responsible for us.

McClean: Then I resign.

Me: If you resign you will be considered a draft dodger and we will have to kill you.

LeForge: I like the sound of that.

Me: (To the Frenchman) You will also be killed for threatening mutiny and for disrespecting the Colonel. The only reason you are still alive is because I'm not yet in charge.

LeForge just barely holds himself back from punching me in the face. He's nearly twice my size. I have no idea why he hesitated.

Me: So, Corporal, are you ready to take charge?

McClean: ...

Me: Sweet is counting on us.

McClean stretches the cold out of his tattooed fingers and half-nods at me.

CHAPTER FIVE
SAWBALL

They call me Crying Hugh Jake because my eyes are always tearing. I tell people it's from allergies.

"Well, why are you still crying then?" LeForge says, straightening his glasses and loading a slag-shot rifle. "There's nothing you can be allergic to out here."

I don't answer him. I'm really not sure why my eyes cry all the time. Not allergies. They just leak.

"We better find the war slut soon," LeForge says to me. "I can handle hunger. I can handle the cold. But I can't go without fucking."

I shake my head at his comment.

"Otherwise I'll have to start fucking McClean," he says, as the Corporal heads our way.

McClean returns with some gear, his teeth chattering and hands shivering. Most of his climate camo has worn off and the temperature must be strong enough to freeze him solid.

"Maybe we should wait until morning," LeForge says, a chill crawling his spine just by witnessing McClean's shivering state.

"No," the Corporal says. "Sweet needs our help."

"But the slut's flesh is synthetic," he says. "It doesn't freeze as quickly as ours."

McClean hands a box of night vision goggles to LeForge and gives me the Lieutenant's wrist monitor.

"Watch for Sweet's life signs," McClean says.

"She's not on here," I say. "Just seven life signs."

"It's got a mile radius," McClean says.

"How'd she wander a mile away from us?" I ask.

"Probably got lost in the snowstorm," McClean says.

"Well, which direction should we go?" I ask.

"North," he says. "We're less than a mile away from the water so we'd pick him up on the monitor if he went south."

"Unless he's dead," LeForge says.

"She's not dead," I tell them.

We suit up for the journey.

"You're not going to need any weapons," McClean tells LeForge and Chauney. "There's nothing out there."

"Maybe you're right about the friendly fire, Corporal," I say, "but those slag-shots weren't ours. I don't think we're alone out here."

"Suit yourselves," he says.

The machine guns are all iced over. We'll have to use slag-shot rifles.

Slag-shot rifles don't shoot regular bullets, they are designed to shoot transforming projectiles, about the size of tampons. There are several different types of projectiles used for a variety of situations. We are taking four different types of slag-shots. Chauney is taking the slam bullets, McClean is taking the stomach bullets, LeForge is taking the library bullets, and I am taking the saw bullets.

"Aw, I wanted the saw bullets," Chauney says.

"Jake's expertise is in saw bullets," McClean says. "Your expertise is in the grenade launcher. The slam bullets are just for backup."

"I never get to use the saw bullets," she says.

"You just want them because they remind you of saw-ball," LeForge says.

Chauney raises her eyebrows, smiles with wide chapped lips, and nods aggressively at his assumption.

"I'm sick for sawball," Chauney says.

Sawball is a sport that is played with two teams of six players. Each team member has a hookbat—a kind of longer thinner version of an aluminum baseball bat with a hook at the top of it.

Each team has six man-shaped figurines they call dodgers, wooden mannequins painted with their team colors, spread out two-by-two on their half of the court. The dodgers each have their own personality: there's the artist and the poet, the teacher and the musician, the philosopher and the terrorist.

There is one sawball. It is hollow metal ball divided into halves. Each half has six pegs. Between the two halves there is a large circular saw that extends three inches out of the ball. It is in constant motion and can only be turned off by the referees.

Players can use their hookbats to latch onto the sawball, which turns their hookbat into what they call the sawbat. Then they use the sawbat to cut away at the opposing team's dodgers. Opposing players will try to hook the sawbat in order to steal the sawball, or they will use the shaft of their bats to block the sawbat from cutting their dodgers.

The object of the game is to use the sawball to cut the opposing team's dodgers into regular people. How this is done depends on which dodger is being sawed. The artist dodger will become a regular person if you saw the paint brush out of his hand. The poet dodger will become a regular person if you cut off his pen. The teacher dodger will become a regular person if you cut the books out of each of his hands. The musician dodger will become a regular person if you cut off his middle finger and his mohawk.

The philosopher dodger will become a regular person if you cut the pipe out of his mouth and the brain out of his head. The terrorist dodger will become a regular person if you cut off the two guns in his hands, and the two bombs on his belt.

At the end of the game, all six dodgers on the losing team's side of the court will look exactly alike.

Points are deducted if a dodger loses a regular appendage. That includes arms, legs, heads, torsos. If a piece of a dodger appendage, such as the paint brush, is not cut off completely then that figurine is still considered a dodger until the rest of the brush is sawed off.

All players are well-armored and are rarely cut with the sawball, but there are some injuries every now and then. Referees will only stop the game if a player is injured, a player's armor is malfunctioning, or the sawball is broken. If a player's hookbat breaks, he must exit the game permanently, leaving his teammates at a huge disadvantage. This has created a high demand for players skilled at sawing aluminum hookbats in half. Though the superstars of the sport are the players who can saw wood quickly and precisely.

Chauney's strength in the game was neither of these, however. She was a mediocre cutter and the musclebound male athletes she would play against were superior defenders and bat-cutters. But she was one of the best sawball stealers in the game. She didn't do much of the cutting, but she could quickly steal the ball from opposing sawbats and pass it across the court to her teammates.

Sawball has been the most beloved planetary sport for years, making Chauney something of a celebrity. But I don't normally think of her as a famous sawball player. I just think of her as Chauney: the Dookaduck girl with three-foot dreadlocks.

McClean insulates his uniform with pages and pages of his poetry.

He's not a very good poet. I've read all ten books of poetry that are in print and it's not like any of those, so it can't be good poetry.

Libraries are mostly technical manuals these days. There are 10 books of poetry and 100 books of fiction. A new novel hasn't been published in over a century. The only way to get a novel published is if it is better than one of the 100. Though, even if a book is better written, how can you compare a new book to a classic?

It's very pointless to write fiction or poetry these days, because of this. Yet you still hear of people doing it, like Mc-Clean. It's a real waste of time if you ask me. If you want to write something, write for television. With almost 22,000 channels there's always a need for television writers.

We leave the officers in their chairs.

"They're getting cold," I say. "Stiff."

Their blinking eyes tell me they aren't dead.

"We won't be gone long," Chauney says.

McClean shrugs.

We head out into the blizzard single file. The snow is hard to walk through, every footstep awkward and clumsy. McClean leads the way. Then myself. Then LeForge. Then Chauney.

The only light emanates behind us, from the officers tent. Looking back, I see three silhouettes through the canvas. All three sitting there perfectly still. They are more like mannequins than real people. Their shadows are cast across the landscape ahead of us, as if they are trying to tell us something with their silence.

"Night vision," McClean says, and we put on our goggles. They don't help much in the snowstorm.

"Use the officers' life signs as a homing point," Mc-Clean says to me.

His voice is so quiet I can barely hear him.

I watch the monitor on my wrist. The triangle of red dots are the officers. The moving line of four dots are us. There aren't any other dots.

"It's bullshit that I'm not an officer," LeForge says to me as we walk. "McClean was born to be a follower, not a leader."

"He's doing fine," I say.

"The only reason I don't get promoted is because of my eyesight," he says. "I've never seen an officer with thick glasses."

"If they thought you were officer-material," I say, "they would have fixed your eyesight for you."

"Then it's because of my French background," he says. "They never promote people with French backgrounds."

"You don't get promoted because you're arrogant, ir-responsible, and disrespectful. The only reason you haven't been put in front of a firing squad for your behavior is because of your disability."

He spits over my shoulder and falls back.

Chauney, LeForge, and I have all been passed up for promotion time and time again.

The reason I haven't been promoted is because of my narcolepsy. I'm always dropping unconscious at unpredictable times. Sometimes when I'm on duty, sometimes during training exercises. It has made my relationship with my commanding officers a very uncomfortable one. And I've become something of a joke with the rest of the soldiers.

Chauney has been passed by for promotion most likely because of her hair or because of her weird religion. They take religion seriously these days. If your commanding officer is of a religion different from yours, you won't be treated very well. Especially if your religion conflicts with theirs. As an atheist, I've always been treated harshly by my superiors. But Chauney has been treated even more harshly than myself. Because her religion isn't only wrong, according to officers, it is also horribly weird. Nobody likes weird people these days.

LeForge has been passed up for a number of reasons, but the main one is probably his disability. He has a mild case of mental retardation, according to a test he once took as a child. There is nothing that pisses him off more than reminding him of this, as it has been something that has hindered him for his entire life. He's not an unintelligent guy. He might have attitude problems but his attitude is probably the result of his upbringing, how he had an excuse to get away with anything he wanted as a child.

Even the handicapped were drafted into the military. Not a single invalid was able to avoid serving. Most of the physically handicapped were given non-combat duties. But the mentally handicapped will usually fight alongside everyone else. They get equal pay, equal responsibility, equal respect, but they usually also get extra benefits such as nap time and less severe punishments when they fuck up.

There are some bodies up ahead, half-buried in the snow.

"Is that where you were attacked?" I ask McClean.

"That's where they killed each other," he says.

"I want to check it out," I say.

He nods.

There are at least a dozen of them we can see. They are spread out pretty far. I don't recognize any of them. Mostly just uniforms and boots are sticking out of the white.

"Look for enemy corpses," I tell LeForge and Chauney.

Chauney breaks off and heads east. LeForge looks around at his feet for a few minutes before giving up.

We inspect the area for several minutes. No enemy bodies. Just our men. Examining the bodies of our fallen allies, we find many of them have saw bullets in them. Or library bullets. The draft dodgers aren't supposed to be advanced enough to create these types of slag-shots.

What if McClean is right? What if there really isn't an enemy force out here? What if they really did just kill each other?

We've never actually been in combat before. We've been in the army our entire lives, and for three years we were stationed at the front lines in North Africa, but I have never seen combat. I have never known anyone who has seen combat. They always talk about soldiers engaging the enemy on television, but I've not seen anything like that in person. My life at war has mostly just been about organization and following orders and doing things as precisely and perfectly as possible.

I'm not even sure exactly what the draft dodger army looks like. What color is their uniform? What flag do they fly?

"What if there never were any draft dodgers? What if the whole war has been a fake?"

"That's dodger talk," LeForge says to me.

"Well, it's true," I say. "None of us have ever seen them."

"You know if an officer heard you say that you'd be in front of a firing squad right now."

"If the war wasn't a lie then why would they be so quick to silence me for saying that?"

"For questioning their authority," he says. "Why would they make up this war, anyway? It's been going on our whole lives!"

"To give us something to do," I say. "Everyone in the world is in the military. We have been trained our entire lives to be soldiers. We are the greatest military force on the face of the planet. But we have no one left to fight."

"We have dodgers to fight," LeForge says. "All the people who refuse to join the army are our enemy."

"We were drafted the day we were born," I say. "We don't dodge the draft as babies. Where did all the draft dodgers come from?"

"See what happens without a proper officer in command!" LeForge says. "We start questioning our faith in freedom!"

"Don't you understand—"

Chauney cuts me off. Her dreads coated in white flakes.

"We found something," she says.

We follow her to McClean.

He's bending over a body in the snow.

"Who is it?" I ask.

"Not who," Chauney says. "What."

It is some kind of dummy, dressed up like a soldier. Plaid clothing stuffed with cotton. McClean hands me a mask. It is a porcelain face that was on top of the dummy's head.

"Where did this come from?" I ask.

They shrug at me. Even LeForge.

"The officers might have set them up," McClean says. "To give the men something to shoot at."

"To make them think there were draft dodgers out here?"

McClean shrugs.

"Or the draft dodgers set it up," Chauney says. "As a scarecrow."

We continue on.

There are still only seven lights on the monitor, but the three officer dots are getting very close to the bottom of the screen.

"If there are draft dodgers out here, how do they live?" I ask them. "What do they eat? How can they survive in this climate?"

"They had a facility in Antarctica," LeForge says. "They can have one here."

"Desperate people always find a way," Chauney says.

After a mile, the snowstorm thickens. We can hardly

see two feet in front of us. I've lost track of camp and we aren't sure we are heading north anymore. I wanted to take a compass, but Chauney said something about how it wouldn't work in the Arctic. She said there was a difference between the north pole and the magnetic north pole, or something like that.

Only our four life signs dot the center of the monitor screen on my wrist. The snow has hardened into rocky ice here and we're finding it impossible to move more than a few feet per minute. We pretty much have to move with all four of our limbs, crawling over ice mounds, soaking our knees. Our rifles smacking us in the chin or stomach whenever we slip and fall.

McClean collapses in front of me and I kneel to help him up, but he won't get up. He curls into a shivering ball.

"McClean!" I say.

The Corporal doesn't respond. His eyes closed tight.

"He's frozen," I tell LeForge behind me.

He's lost all of his climate camo and his pages of poetry have become wet against his skin.

"We need to warm him up," Chauney says.

She huddles us around him. Even LeForge joins. Probably because he is freezing himself. We pack together into a bundle of warmth, the snow wrapping us up in a thick white blanket. I fall asleep.

The snow clears as I wake. Chauney pushes out of the white powder and steps away from us. I follow her. Le-Forge stays behind, holding McClean as tightly as he can, like a long lost brother. The storm rushes away from us, heading north. We take off our night vision goggles. The moon and stars are out. The sky is a dark blue.

"It's beautiful," Chauney says, hugging her grenade launcher like a teddy bear.

I wish I was her grenade launcher.

To the north, the ice is flat. It reflects the sky like water. A frozen lake. The surface might be dangerous that way. The last thing we need is to break the ice and go underwater.

I think Chauney knows I'm in love with her. Whenever I'm looking at her she always catches me. Whenever she brushes against me or sits next to me, she can tell I get aroused. But she doesn't ever blush when she catches me, so I'm sure she doesn't feel the same way. She probably thinks it's cute that I have a crush on her, but probably doesn't care enough to confront me about it. It probably wouldn't be awkward unless she asked me about it.

Being a serious soldier, and being the famous celebrity sawball player that she is, I doubt she'd ever want to have anything to do with me. She smiles chapped lips at me from behind a dreadlock hanging in her face like a bang. I blush and look away from her.

At first I think it's an illusion in the storm. But, as the storm clears ahead, I see it take shape in the distance.

The smile falls off of Chauney's face. She sees it too.

A city on the ice.

CHAPTER SIX
THE LOST CITY

McClean and LeForge rise to their feet and join us.

"What is that?" McClean asks.

The city is small. Maybe twenty skyscrapers and a handful of smaller buildings, all the color of ice. There are no lights coming from the buildings. No traffic in the streets. No movement or sounds at all. It just looks dead. Long dead.

"Let's go find out," I say.

We wipe off the snow and head toward the city, our slag-shot rifles at the ready.

"Think Sweet is in there?" LeForge says.

"There's no life signs," I tell him, looking at my wrist monitor. "This city is deserted."

"Life signs can be cloaked," Chauney says.

"Yeah, if they cool their body temperatures," I say. "But out here that would be suicide."

"Fall in," McClean says.

His voice shaking, hands frozen against his rifle.

We quiet down for the approach ...

The moon is bright enough to illuminate the way, reflecting the entire sky against the smooth clear ice. It is like we are walking on a mirror. McClean nearly slips onto his butt when he looks down. He steps to the side, pointing his rifle at the ground, then continues on.

I look in the ice to see what startled him. There is a car

down there, frozen in the ice. A baby blue Cadillac from the 1950s. It looks to be floating down there in the water, floating in space.

As we continue, we find more cars frozen in the ice. Some closer to the surface, some so deep they look like toys. Many different makes from many different eras. One of the cars has its headlights on, brightening the under-ice world for us.

There are more things than cars under there. We see tables, chairs, stop signs, fire hydrants, doors, lamps, dog houses, bookshelves full of books, and dozens and dozens of television sets—all of them turned on with bright static on their screens. I look at the others and they look at me. But none of us can think of anything to say.

Stepping through the light of television static issuing from our feet, we arrive at the first of the city buildings. It is iced over. Dark.

I touch it to make sure it's real.

"Be on your guard," McClean says softly.

The streets are the same smooth ice, only there are more items frozen beneath: train tracks, airplanes, phone booths, traffic lights, a football stadium.

We walk through the ghost city. There's no one here. I check the monitor every other minute. No life signs.

"These buildings ..." Chauney says, examining closer. "They're all made of ice."

I disagree.

"Igloo skyscrapers?" LeForge asks.

She nods her dreads.

There seems to be more life beneath the ice than above. The streets are empty. The windows are empty. Just frozen buildings. The place is haunted.

McClean takes the words right out of my mouth when he says, "Something's wrong."

"Let's go inside," McClean says.

We step across the street, slowly so we don't slip, our footsteps make an echoing clack against the surface that sounds like someone's drumming on glass.

The door is frozen shut. It looks like it's made of ice, but I'm sure it's just caked in ice. It takes LeForge a good ram with his shoulder to break it open. He spills into the lobby and hits a man in the waist.

LeForge screams and punches the man's head off.

"What is it?" Chauney asks from the back, trying to see over our shoulders.

It wasn't really a man. Just another dummy.

The lobby is filled with dummies. Maybe thirty mannequins in poses. Some are at the front desk. Some are sitting on couches reading newspapers. Some are positioned as if they are chatting at the elevator.

"Peculiar ..." LeForge says, rubbing his chin.

"This isn't what I was expecting," I say.

We wander the building. The floor in here is linoleum and it's easier to walk. It's also a bit warmer, but not much. All of the walls and furniture are white. Only the clothes on the mannequins have color.

Chauney and I separate from the others and take stairs up to the next floor.

"What do you think this place is?" Chauney asks.

"Some kind of museum, I'd say."

"What kind of museum would they put in the Arctic?"

I shrug, then say, "Or maybe it was some kind of housing development from a long time ago that was never completed. They put mannequins up to represent people, give a better view of their plan for when investors came to check the place out. It was probably abandoned ages ago after they lost funding."

"What about all those cars under the ice?"

"Maybe there was an accident. The street could have split open and everything fell underwater. Maybe that's how they lost their investors and had to leave this place."

"You don't think the draft dodgers built this?"

I shake my head.

"If there really ever were any draft dodgers they never came here," I say. "This place is dead." I hold up my wrist monitor. "No life signs at all. Perhaps the government recently got information on this place and told the Colonel to take his men to check it out. Just in case there were draft dodgers hiding out here."

"There could still be a dodger base somewhere," she says. "It could be under the ice where monitors can't read."

"I doubt it," I say.

"Then what about Sweet?" she says. "You don't think she was taken prisoner?"

"Sweet got lost in the storm," I say. "I'm sure she's dead."

CHAPTER SEVEN
HONEY EAR

I awake to bullets firing.

The loud ceramic pops of the slag-shot rifles and there's also machine gun fire out there.

What's happening?

"Come on," Chauney cries, trying to lift me up off the stairs. "You picked the worst time to be narcoleptic."

There really are draft dodgers out here!

I look at my life sign monitor ...

"Wait ..."

There are still only four life signs.

Chauney races up to the next floor and breaks out a window. McClean and LeForge are now in the street. Snipers are firing down at them from the roof of an adjacent building.

"You were right," I tell her. "They are able to cloak their life signs somehow."

Chauney launches a grenade at the snipers across the street and the roof explodes. The top corner of the building shatters into ice cubes that rain into the street.

The building really is made of ice ...

"Got 'em," she says.

A bullet pierces Chauney's shoulder. She drops to the floor.

I turn around. The room is filled with more mannequins. It's a kind of restaurant and lounge. I don't see the gun man yet, but he's in the room with us.

The bullet didn't go very deep. Chauney pulls it out and shows it to me.

"Ice?" I say.

It's not a bullet. It's an icicle.

The sniper fires at us again and misses. The bullet shatters against the wall. I pull Chauney into the stairwell.

"Take him alive," she says, handing me her slag-shot rifle filled with slam bullets.

"I'll try," I tell her, wrapping my rifle over my shoulder and grabbing hers.

I crawl across the floor on my belly through the forest of mannequins, under the tables, as quietly as I can. The sniper doesn't fire yet. White table cloth in my face.

Footsteps.

He's coming closer, toward the window. Probably thinks we went down the stairs.

Crap. Chauney is defenseless over there. She can't fire her grenade launcher at that range. Better not let him get by me.

The footsteps get closer, passing tables and mannequins.

Once I see the legs, I hop to my feet and fire a slam-shot, throwing the sniper across a table. He takes the display plates, plastic floral center piece, and several mannequins with him.

Slam bullets are designed to knock down an enemy or group of enemies without killing them. After they leave the gun, slam-shots only go ten feet and then open up into an airbag that knock the attacker down, usually unconscious. You have to get the right range or they'll be as harmless as balloons.

Before I can get to him, a bullet hits me in the face and I fall to the ground.

There's a second sniper.

I race across the floor, crawling, holding my face together. The pain is freezing. Blood gushes onto the linoleum and the socks of the mannequins.

Once I break free of the mannequin jungle, I'm showered with bullets overhead. I scurry across the tiles and leap into the stairwell, sliding on my belly down a few steps. There's a pain in my arm. It is all bloody, but I'm not sure if I've been hit with another bullet or not.

Chauney isn't in the stairwell. I look at my wrist. All four life signs are spread out. Everyone fled from the building in different directions.

In the lobby, I toss Chauney's rifle and ready my slag-shot with saw rounds, knocking mannequins out of my way to get behind the front desk.

My face is pounding. I spit globs of blood onto the floor, next to the clerk mannequin's shoes. Pieces of teeth are in the blood. I reach into a pouch on my belt and retrieve a small jar containing a honey ear. I scoop out the gooey liquid and wipe it into my left earlobe.

The honey ear contains a chemical that enhances your sense of sound. It basically becomes an extension of your earlobe and amplifies sound waves. I can hear the footsteps of the snipers coming down the stairs after me. I can hear gun shots far in the distance.

Examining my wound ...

The ice bullet went into my mouth and pierced through my cheek, shattering two of my teeth and I think it cracked my jawbone a little. Another bullet grazed my right arm.

The snipers are in the lobby now, walking carefully through the mannequins.

I'm not an expert with the honey ear. Supposedly, with the right training, you're supposed to be able to visualize exactly where your enemy is standing by the sound of his footsteps. You can have the acute senses of a bat. If I was expertly trained, I could take out these two no problem. I'm almost a master with the saw-shots. That combined with honey ear mastery and my enemies wouldn't last two seconds.

But, instead, I think I'll stay on the cautious side. I don't want to risk getting any more injured. They will move on eventually.

I try to breathe as quietly as possible, watching the four dots on my monitor spread further and further apart.

CHAPTER EIGHT
DISAPPEARING LIGHTS

I wake up. Must have fallen asleep again. I don't know how long I've been out. Not picking up any sound through my honey ear except the sound of my breath.

Looking at my wrist monitor ...

There's only one red light left. Mine.

Shit ...

The others might be dead. Chauney might be dead. Or maybe they just went off the grid. They could have gone back to camp.

I look out into the lobby. The mannequins stare back at me.

No snipers. No draft dodgers.

Draft dodgers. I can't believe I doubted our government. They are as cruel and as cunning as the television said. I have to get back to camp. Chauney could be waiting for me. Or maybe she's lost in the snow and needs my help. I don't care about the others, but if they killed Chauney ...

Outside, the streets are loud with wind. It's like a thundering hammer against my eardrums. I have to scoop the honey out of my ear so that I don't go deaf. The streets are empty. I don't see the enemy anywhere.

There are probably snipers watching this building so I better move fast. Once I'm halfway across the street, a thick blizzard crushes through the city like a tidal wave and knocks me off my feet. I get up and move as fast as I can on the ice. This blizzard might actually be a blessing if it hides me from the snipers.

I get all the way out of the city before they start firing at me. Just one sniper. He misses by about a hundred feet. Might have just been shooting at my shadow stretched far across the glassy ice.

I stagger through the storm, back to camp, not taking my eyes off my wrist monitor.

I'm still the only red dot.

Back into the jagged ice terrain, I should be able to see their life signs by now.

I continue, pulling myself through the storm. No sign of them. I go for a mile. No red lights. I have to be going the wrong way. Must have gotten lost in the storm.

The wind peels the last of my climate camo off of my face and my ears feel like they are ready to crack. My eyes water, creating a layer of ice on my cheeks that feels like a collection of razor cuts.

Red lights. I see them. My face is ready to burn off in the wind, but I'll be able to make it back to camp. I fall to my knees.

Only three of them. The triangle of officers.

The others didn't make it.

I continue on.

I've got to get back to the shelter soon or I'm dead.

I look at the monitor. Just half a mile away.

"What a minute ..."

One of the red lights is missing. There are only two up on the screen now. One of them must have died.

Another red light disappears from the screen.

"Shit ..."

Something is killing them. Could be the cold ...

Only one red light left.

I see the camp up ahead. Don't need the monitor anymore. Don't want to see the last red light go out ...

The wind dies down before I reach the camp.

The snow is still falling, even thicker than before. But now it falls slowly. Delicate powder. There is only one silhouette casting a shadow through the canvas tent across the ground. The other two are missing. I open the tent flaps with the barrel of my gun to find Lieutenant Chase staring back at me.

He is still in the same spot as he has been, staring in the same direction as before. But now he is alone. The Colonel and Major have vanished. They must have been killed and carried off. But there isn't any blood ... Strangled maybe. The enemy might have seen me coming and went into hiding.

"Lieutenant, we have to hide you," I tell him.

He just stares.

I go to pick him up. He's as stiff as a corpse.

I touch his face ... It's frozen solid. I look at my life sign monitor. I am the only red light. This man is dead.

Wait ...

His skin. It's not right ...

I touch it. It is made of porcelain. His face breaks off in my hand. Inside of his head, there is only cotton. This isn't the Lieutenant. It is just another dummy.

Whoever left him here isn't coming back.

I warm myself with the lamp. It isn't much but I'm able to defrost before going back out there. I make a scarf out of the Lieutenant's uniform and wrap it around my face. Then insulate my uniform with his dummy's cotton stuffing. It'll also work as a temporary bandage for my face wound.

There's still a chance that the others are lost out there in the snow, trying to find their way back to camp. If they're out there, I'll find them. Then we'll wipe these draft dodgers off the face of the planet.

CHAPTER NINE
SAW SOLDIER

Back into the storm.

I try to collect some more ammunition on the way out, but all of the supply crates have been coated in three inches of ice that I'm unable to crack with the butt of my gun. I've got four packs of saw-shots, but that's not going to be enough. I'll have to collect arms from the enemy as I take them down.

There are fresh tracks of footprints in the snow, heading toward the city. The three who hit the camp. Or maybe it's McClean, LeForge, and Chauney. Perhaps they've found some of the enemy's cloaking devices and I'm unable to read them on my monitor. I've got to hope.

I get out onto the frozen lake and check the monitor. There is a second red light up ahead, somewhere in the city. Someone is still alive.

There's hope. It could be Chauney.

I race across the ice, avoiding the light of the television static underneath. The snow fall has now made it easier to move on the ice. I can now run without slipping.

The enemy soldiers are waiting for me. Their ice bullets crack the ground beneath me and behind me. They can't see me in this thick snowfall. They're shooting blind, probably using a life signs monitor and aiming for my red dot.

The saw bullets are useless at this distance in the open.

The advantage of saw-shots is that they ricochet when they hit hard surfaces, and cut through everything of a softer material (such as wood or flesh), and they do not lose momentum no matter how many walls they bounce off of or how many people they cut through. They can self-propel themselves for two minutes, then the blades will stop moving and they will drop to the ground.

The bullets look like two miniature circular saws, a smaller one stacked on top of a slightly larger one. Like a quarter stacked on top of a half-dollar.

I am quite proficient at firing saw-shots, because I was good at playing pool. The technique is the same. I'm not a mathematical genius like most saw-shot rifleman. I just can feel angles. I don't know how to describe it, but I can tell exactly where my bullets are going to hit without having to do equations in my head. I can also usually visualize the path of the bullet for the full two minutes until it dies and lands on the ground. They call it seeing the lines. I'm great at seeing the lines. Not always, but usually. I'm also very good at dodging out of the way of the bullets when they come back at me. I can usually predict when and if they will come back.

Most people using saw-shots tend to get killed by their own bullets. No matter how expert they are at hitting targets in the training sessions, they tend to either miscalculate the trajectories under pressure or just can't duck out of the way in time. Very few people are skilled enough to use saw-shots. I've always been proud to be one of them.

There are snipers in one of the dark icy buildings ahead, three stories above me. I shoot just one bullet. The gun makes a loud pop and the bullet whirs into the room with them. Their firing stops as the tiny saws bounce against walls and cut through everything in their path. I assume I got them. They are no longer at the window. I can't visualize the bullet's trajectory when I can't see inside the room, but I'm sure I got them.

I continue on, into the street. The red dot is just slightly north and a few buildings east. Once I get into the main intersection I am bombarded with icicle-shots from all sides. I dart into the closest building. It's some kind of tavern inside, frozen like the interior of the hotel. Mannequins are sitting in stools at the bar. A bartender mannequin holds a bottle of gin.

Ducking to the floor and peering out of a window, I see enemy soldiers on the street in the distance. Once they are at the proper angle, I break out the glass and fire at the building across from them. The saw bullet zig-zags from building to building, carving the group to pieces. So far, they're no match for me. Just two bullets and I've killed at least a dozen of them.

I exit out the back door. The red dot isn't moving. Whoever it is must have found a safe place to hide. Or has been captured. After a block, I can see the building up ahead where my comrade must have taken refuge. Icicles rip through the snow at me. Many troops are coming from the direction I am headed. I'll have to fight my way through.

I pass a coffee shop and get just a glimpse of movement inside. A bullet shatters the shop's window. I drop to the ground. It missed me. Before it can fire again, I squeeze a saw bullet into the shop, then wait two minutes for the bullet to rip him to pieces.

Two minutes pass and the bullet dies. I peak into the window. Lying on the ground, his body was shredded. Many mannequins in the coffee shop have also been shredded. Their stuffing floating in the air like it's snowing on the inside.

I climb in through the window to examine the sniper's body ...

Shit ...

I've missed him. I hit only mannequins.

He must have gone out the back door.

But the mannequin I thought was the sniper is holding a rifle ...

"Tricky bastard," I say to the stuffing-snow.

The sniper must have been wearing a mask to blend in with the mannequins. Clever way to get the drop on me. He moves his leg. He's still alive, trying to get to his feet. I kick his gun away and stomp on his chest to force him back to the ground. Then I rip off his mask.

It's not a mask ...

The porcelain face in my hand writhes. I look down at it. Its mouth is opening and closing as if to talk. I look down at the sniper. His head is filled with cotton. Just like the Lieutenant. It still moves. Its hands feeling around its head in search of the face.

He isn't a human dressed as a dummy. He is a dummy. A living doll.

I smash its head and the body goes limp.

As I turn around to leave, one of the surviving mannequins comes to life. It picks up the sniper's rifle and aims it at me. I jump out of the window before the bullet is fired.

I scatter across the ice twenty feet before I realize I am surrounded by enemy soldiers. Getting a close look at them ... their faces are made of porcelain. All of them are doll people. This whole city, they are all living dolls.

CHAPTER TEN
BURNING BLOOD

Perhaps out of desperation, perhaps out of fear, I now find myself firing madly at the soldiers around me, spinning in a circle to get them all. Saw-shots cut through the closest ones and then cut through those behind them. Stuffing puffs out of their wounds and they tumble to the ground.

I re-load my weapon and look at my wrist monitor. The red dot is still up ahead.

More doll people come at me. Not just soldiers. Now there are civilians—business men, janitors, mothers, children, cooks, butchers—coming out of the shops and apartment buildings, carrying knives, hammers, baseball bats. They are all silent. Only the clacking of their faces against their hands makes noise.

I charge through the street, firing in every direction, toward the building with the red dot. Dozens of saw-shots flying through the air chaotically. I have fired too many to visualize their paths. Mini-saws fly over my head or past my feet, coming from all sides. And I keep firing more into the doll people as I run, slipping on icy patches of snow.

The building is just up ahead. It is some kind of warehouse.

A mad butcher doll, obese with a white apron, comes at me from behind with a large cleaver. When I get to the door, I fire at the wall in front of me and duck. The saw-shot bounces against the wall, whirs over my head, and decapitates the mad butcher.

Its over-stuffed body plops into the snow.

Looking back, there aren't any others following me. They must have lost me in the snowfall. I look down on the monitor. The red dot is right next to my red dot. My comrade, perhaps Chauney, is just a few feet away from me. Separated by a single icy wall.

Yes, I think it is Chauney. I can feel it.

The door is locked. I back away from it, hide behind some steps. Chauney must have barricaded the door. I can't knock. It could give our position away. Or, if she's a prisoner, I could be walking into a trap.

Better find another way in.

I circle the building. Doll people are out wandering in the streets. Probably searching for me. But they don't look like they are hunting. They just stroll along the sidewalks casually, like they're walking home from work.

Creeping through the snow, I get to a window and peer in. Can't see anybody. It's dark in there. I go to the front door and am surprised to find it unlocked.

Must be a trap.

I ready my slag-shot rifle and enter, dropping to the floor. My wounded jaw hits the ice and sends a stabbing pain through my face. Nobody shoots me.

I stand and go to the next room, to the red dot. It is too dark. Mostly shadows.

"Something's wrong," a voice says from the shadows.

It isn't Chauney. It is McClean.

I go to him. He's naked, sitting in the dark, tattooing his knees. His entire body is coated in tattoos, very scraggy homemade tattoos. A couple look like dragons, but the rest just look like sloppy ink marks. Most of them are fresh, created since we arrived in the Arctic. Large portions of his skin look infected, perhaps from not sterilizing his needle or perhaps it's ink poisoning.

"McClean?"

He stops tattooing his knees and begins tattooing his back blindly, rapidly poking an inky sewing needle into his skin.

"It's so hot," he says, rubbing his body as if trying to take off more of his clothes, trying to take off a layer of skin. "It's too hot to breathe."

"You must have hypothermia," I say. "You're so freezing you think you're hot."

I've got to warm him up. Maybe with body heat. When I touch his skin, I notice he really is hot. Very hot. There are droplets of climate camo in the ink vial. There's not really any climate camo on his skin, but I don't think it's been rubbed off. I think the camo has been absorbed into his bloodstream, heating up his body to an unnatural temperature.

"Cut it out," I say to him, taking the ink away.

He reaches out to poke me with the needle, but I snatch his hand and take that away, too. "You're poisoning yourself."

He rolls over and rubs his chest against the ice to cool down. It doesn't seem to help.

"What's going on?" I ask. "Where were you?"

He just shakes his head at me.

"Where are the others?"

He shrugs.

After an hour, he calms down. Much of the climate camo

sweats out of his bloodstream. His mind has probably been poisoned by the stuff. He's unable to keep his head up straight. He doesn't speak. His only sign of life is when he squeezes my ankle as I try to put his uniform back on.

I watch the window, just waiting for the doll people to attack. Nobody attacks. There isn't a soldier in sight. Just civilians, strolling along the sidewalks like stiff-jointed specters. No expressions on their white porcelain faces. No reason for them to be walking about.

"What the hell are they?" I ask myself.

"Ghosts," McClean says from behind.

I look at him. His eyes are closed and he's leaning against the wall.

"Ghosts?"

He doesn't respond.

I look back at the street. It is now empty.

The next person to walk down the sidewalk is LeForge. He's walking casually, carrying his gun, and spitting over his shoulder.

I look at my monitor. There's not a third red dot. He shouldn't be here. Unless there really is a device that hides life signs ...

Racing out of the building and into the street, I call out, "LeForge!"

He turns around, sees me. Smiles. I wave him over. He looks left and right and then crosses the road, pushing his glasses up onto his face. An icicle pierces across his shoulder before he gets to me. He crouches down and races forward. Soldiers are firing at us from around the corner.

I pull him into the warehouse and empty a clip of saw shots into the street, killing two of them and creating a wall of ricocheting fire that the rest will not be able to cross.

"Holy fuck," LeForge cries. "Where the hell have you been?"

"I went back to camp," I told him.

"This little shit ran off and left me alone," he says, kicking the Corporal.

"Are you wounded?" I ask him.

He shrugs. There are holes in his uniform but he appears to be fine.

"Where's Chauney?" I ask the Frenchman as he does push-ups on the ground.

"She's dead," he says.

"What happened?" I ask.

"I don't know," he says, doing sit-ups now. "I found her body in the storm."

"Are you sure?"

He shrugs at me and starts doing jumping jacks.

"What the hell are you doing?" I ask.

"Trying to keep warm," he says. "Exercise will keep you from freezing to death."

"You're just going to rub off the last of your climate camo," I say.

"I ran out of that days ago."

I look at my wrist monitor. He's still not registering.

"Are you wearing some kind of cloaking device?" I ask.

"Huh?"

"Your life signs aren't registering." I show him my wrist. "How are you hiding your body temperature?"

"Let me see that." He pulls my arm to his face and flares his nostrils as he adjusts his glasses.

"It's broken," he says, giving me back my arm.

"How do you know?" I ask.

"Because I'm standing right in front of you, moron."

I go back to the window. The doll people are crowding around the building. Two of them are soldiers, rallying the rest of the citizens in the area to surround us, corner us.

"Shit," I say. "They're coming."

LeForge comes to the window.

"Barricade the doors," he says.

"Sure we want to trap ourselves in here?" I ask.

"I'm not going anywhere," he says. "It's fucking cold out there."

CHAPTER ELEVEN
LIBRARY SOLDIER, STOMACH SOLDIER

The doll people attack the doors and windows with bats and knives. I reload my rifle with my last clip of saw-shots and fire at them from the window. LeForge supports the door with his body weight. McClean watches the back doors. They are solid iron with a strong lock connecting them together. He takes off his shirt, coils it into a rope, and ties it to the door handles to reinforce the lock. The cold still doesn't bother him. LeForge frowns at the bloody tattoos covering his skin. He didn't realize the Corporal had so many.

My saw-shots slice through several of the doll people at once, but they ricochet in another direction when they hit the wall of the building across the street. It's almost a waste of my bullets.

The front door cracks apart, barely held together by the furniture and LeForge's body. There are spaces where the dolls can get their arms through, stabbing at the French-man, grabbing for his flesh. LeForge rips a doll arm off of one of them, and tosses it away. Stuffing pokes out of the arm as it wriggles on the floor.

"What the fuck?" he says, as if he just now realizes they aren't human.

I try ripping off their limbs or heads as well when they try to climb through the window. I don't want to waste my saw shots, so I get a baseball bat from one of them and begin smashing their porcelain faces or crushing their fingers into cotton fluff.

"Hand me my rifle," LeForge says.

He's unable to bend down to pick it up while holding the door.

McClean picks it up and hands it to him, and LeForge fires a library bullet into the arm of one of the doll people. The doll falls back and thrashes in the crowd.

Library bullets are shaped like tiny books that flap through the air when fired. The usefulness of these bullets is that they will kill a person no matter where they hit, because the bullet continues flapping inside of the person, chewing up their insides. Even if a person is hit in the foot, the library-shot will crawl up the inside of the limb until it gets into the torso, convulsing and slashing its way through the entire body for two minutes until it dies.

Usually the most sadistic soldiers specialize in library-shots. Sometimes they are known as Library Soldiers, as I am sometimes known as a Saw Soldier. LeForge fits the profile of a typical Library Soldier.

LeForge continues shooting their limbs with library bullets, laughing as the tiny books chew through the doll arms, spitting out cotton and chunks of porcelain. He probably wishes they were made of flesh, wishes they could create a gory scene for him, wishes they could feel the pain he was giving them.

He drops the gun and falls back as a volley of icicles pierce into his chest. Blood sprays across the white wood furniture barricading the door. Instead of arms poking through the space in the door, two rifles had poked through and shot him at point blank range. I slam my bat down across the rifles in the door, bending the barrels an inch downwards, rendering them useless. I fire a couple saw rounds through the hole before they fall back.

LeForge is still standing there, fingering his wounds.

"You okay?" I ask.

He shrugs.

"It's cold," he says, poking his finger into a bullet hole.

"You're in shock," I tell him.

"No, it's still in me," he says. "It's freezing."

He widens the hole and digs out the ice bullet.

"What the fuck?" he says. "I can't feel anything but cold."

I hold back the front door as the crowd tries to break through with even more fury. I fire saw-rounds across the room at the doll people crawling in through the window.

"I'm numb," LeForge says, ripping open the skin on his chest like he's ripping open a shirt.

"What the hell are you doing?" I say.

LeForge pulls a wad of cotton out of his belly. He examines it casually. Intestines spill out of his torso, revealing more cotton. He is stuffed with it, like the Lieutenant.

"He's one of them," McClean cries.

LeForge shrugs as he tosses the ball of stuffing over his shoulder and turns around.

McClean picks up his rifle.

"McClean," I yell, as he fires a stomach-round into the Frenchman's face.

The stomach bullet is like a small water balloon filled with acid. It explodes against LeForge's face. The Frenchman shrieks as his flesh burns rapidly. His entire head melts off of his neck before he has a chance to hit the ground.

"What the hell?" I say, re-loading my rifle with the last of my slags.

"Move," McClean says.

"Take the window," I tell him.

"Move," he says.

I dodge out of the way just before he fires a stomach-shot through the hole in the door, showering acid onto the crowd.

I go to the window and break porcelain faces with the butt of my gun. McClean takes the front entrance.

"McClean, be careful," I say to him.

But he isn't careful. He fires another shot and it misses the hole, splashing against the door's barricade instead. The wood melts and cracks apart. The Corporal backs up, watching as the doll people break through the melting wood as if it's now made of paper.

"Let's get out of here," I tell McClean, but he's already out of the back door and running shirtless down the street.

I fire the last of my saw shots as the living mannequins fill the room. Crawling across the floor, I get LeForge's rifle and pull myself outside.

McClean isn't in sight. Not sure which direction he went. I look at my monitor. It's dissolving. I look down at my clothes. They are also dissolving. I must have been crawling through the acid.

"Shit." I take off the wrist computer and my shirt.

The mob comes around the corner and charges me, stiff mechanical movements with expressionless faces rushing through the snow. I fire LeForge's slag-shot rifle like a machine gun into the mob, dozens of tiny flapping books flitter through the air at them. They are like butterflies made of razor blades.

The dolls crumble to the ground as the bullets hit them, chewing the stuffing out of their clothes. I fire until not a single one of them is still standing. Then I remove some of their shredded garments and drape them over me for warmth. Examining them in the nude. They have all the parts of real humans. They have breasts, dicks, vaginas. But their flesh is made of cloth, stuffed with cotton. Their faces, hands, and feet made of white ceramic.

I don't catch up with McClean in time.

Up ahead, I find him kneeling in the street. He's been shot in the side, bleeding onto the ice, and several of the doll soldiers are standing over him with their rifles in his face. He puts his hands on the back of his head and cries at them. They lift him to his feet and escort him away.

I dodge into a nearby building. There are several dead mannequins lying on the floor here, riddled with bullets. Machine gun bullets. Only one mannequin is still standing, holding the rifle.

"Attention!" it says.

I know that voice ...

Stepping closer, I get a better look at the doll man with the machine gun. It is Colonel Dupont. He's still wearing his uniform, but his face and hands are now porcelain.

"Private Jake, why aren't you on the front lines?" he asks. "We must eliminate all draft dodgers!"

He is completely still. Only his mouth is moving, slightly. But it doesn't quite move with his words. Like his voice is being badly dubbed.

"How many men do we have left?" he says.

"I think I'm the last," I tell him. "Corporal McClean was captured by the enemy."

"Very well," he says. "Then we will have to take out the enemy ourselves."

I back away from him.

"Fall in, Private," he says.

I continue moving.

"This is insubordination," he says. "Disobeying orders is a capital offense."

I raise the slag-shot rifle and fire the last bullet at him. It hits him in the stomach. He rips open his uniform and unzips his chest, then pulls the flapping bullet out of him by a razor wing. He tosses it aside.

"Mutineers are shot on site!" he says, aiming his rifle at me.

His head shatters before he gets a chance to fire. Somebody hit him with a chair from behind.

I look up at my rescuer. It is Chauney. She is still alive.

"Come on," she says, waving me over.

I follow her up a staircase to an empty apartment. She locks the door behind us.

"You're safe here," she says, sitting me down on a white couch. "Relax."

"I thought you were dead," I say.

She shakes her dreadlocks at me.

"LeForge saw your body in the snow," I say.

She shrugs.

"They got McClean," I tell her. "We have to help him."

She sits down next to me. "Don't worry. He'll be fine."

"They killed the others," I say.

She hushes me.

"They were only defending themselves," she says. "They don't want to hurt anyone."

"What do you mean? You spoke to them?"

"Yes," she says. "They say that they just want to live their own lives. They want to be free."

"You mean, those animated dolls out there are really the draft dodgers?"

She nods her head.

"How is that possible?"

She hushes me again.

"Don't worry, we're not in any danger. They'll let us stay here. We can be together forever."

"Chauney, what's wrong with you?" I ask.

She takes off her clothes. Her long dreads brushing against her skin give her gooseflesh, cold metal chains hardening her nipples.

"I know you want to be with me," she says, climbing onto the table and standing over me. "I know you used to have the war slut change into me so you could pretend you were making love with me."

She squats down and rubs the wound on my cheek like it's erotic. She sticks her finger through the hole and fucks it slowly.

"The funny thing is," she says, "I used to have Sweet change into you as well."

I pull her finger out of my cheek hole and stare her in her orange yarn eyes. "Really?"

She grins at me.

"I've been in love with you for the longest time," she says. "But you know how it is in the military. We can't fraternize when at war. Soldiers can't fall in love. But the war is over now and we're in a place where we are allowed to love, where we can live freely."

"Live here?" I ask. "In the Arctic? With these doll people?"

"It's really not that bad," she says. "It's freedom. We'll be free to do whatever we want. It is a huge price to pay, but it's better to live badly and be free than live in wealth as a slave."

She removes my clothes and wraps her body around me, kisses my neck, warms my cold flesh with her hot black skin.

"Be with me," she whispers into my ear.

I submit to her warmth, press my face against her neck.

"Can we survive here?" I ask.

She wipes the tears out of my eyes.

"We'll be well taken care of," she says.

She sucks my tongue into her mouth, keeping her eyes open so she can stare into me with her tan-orange eyes. Then pulls away and has me suck on one of her dreads like a dick. The hair entwined with metal is rough on my tongue, and it tastes absolutely terrible, but I can tell it turns her on so I pretend to enjoy it. I'm careful not to hurt myself on the small hook that she attached to the end of the dread.

She pulls on the hook so that it slips through the hole in my cheek, and then she pulls on it.

"Look, I've caught a fish," she says.

She stands up and tugs on her dread until I come to her. She pulls me across the room to a table and lays me across it.

"I like this fish," she says, climbing on top of me.

She takes the hook out of my mouth and attaches it to the edge of the table. Then she hooks all of her dreads to all of the edges of the table, like a web trapping me beneath her. With her last two dreads, she tangles one of my wrists around each of them before hooking them to the table.

Then, completed bound by her hair, she slips my penis inside of her and fucks me. The table is cold but her warmth is calming. She closes her eyes and licks the blood from my face, stinging the wound with her peppery tongue.

I know it's really Sweet, but I want to go on pretending. At least until we are done.

CHAPTER TWELVE
NEW DAY

The morning comes.

I wake up in a white bed, not sure how I got here.

It's cold, but not so bad. I can walk around in the nude without getting a chill.

Sweet is sitting in a chair, watching the sunrise, watching the doll people stroll casually in the street, cleaning up after their dead. She is still pretending to be Chauney.

I sit down beside her. Something is wrong. Her skin has become pale.

"Are you okay?"

I feel her skin. It's cold and stiff.

She wipes my hand away.

"It's okay," she says. "It's just the change."

"What change?" I ask.

"We're becoming like them," she says.

She smiles at me. The lips on her face curl her cheeks awkwardly.

I want to ask her what she means by that, but I don't have to. I can tell her skin is turning to porcelain.

I shake my head at her.

"It's the only way," she says. "It's the only way we can be free."

I feel my own face. It is also getting stiff.

"We're going to become dolls?" I ask.

"They can't read our life signs from satellite this way," she says. "You said you wanted to be with me forever. It's a fair trade."

"I don't want to be like them," I say.

"Trust me," she says. "You'll be much happier this way."

Our skin becomes porcelain later in the day. I'm not ready to face the other doll people. Not ready to apologize for the carnage I've caused.

We make love again, in the bedroom, but it just isn't the same. Our bodies are cold. Our flesh feels like fabric. Our heads clack together whenever they touch. And my penis feels only cotton inside of her.

There is no emotion in her porcelain face anymore. Her facial features just look painted onto her head. And I'm sure my face looks exactly the same. I'm scared to look at myself in the mirror.

As we make love, I stare up at the ceiling. I don't understand any of this. Why do these people believe this is a better way of life? They live in the harshest environment on the planet. They have to live within the bodies of dolls. They can't possibly enjoy anything. Not sex, not food, not drink. Their lives can't possibly be fulfilling. Why do these people bother? Why did they dodge the draft? Why didn't they just submit to the government like everyone else?

I'm still able to have an orgasm, but I don't understand how.

THE END

THE ART OF ED MIRONIUK

**48 full color pages of kinky and kutie pin-up
girls with a rough and ready attitude
hand signed with original one of a kind sketch
$40**

http://edmironiuk.bigcartel.com/

"Fetish pinup girls that are as interesting and strange as they
are sexy. The more you see of Ed Mironiuk's art, the more it
will attach itself to you. This book is a must-buy."

Carlton Mellick III

ABOUT THE AUTHOR

Carlton Mellick III is one of the leading authors in the new *Bizarro* genre uprising. Since 2001, his surreal counterculture novels have drawn an international cult following despite the fact that they have been shunned by most libraries and corporate bookstores. He lives in Portland, OR, the bizarro fiction mecca.

Visit him online at **www.carltonmellick.com**

Bizarro books

CATALOG   SPRING 2011

Bizarro Books publishes under the following imprints:

www.rawdogscreamingpress.com

www.eraserheadpress.com

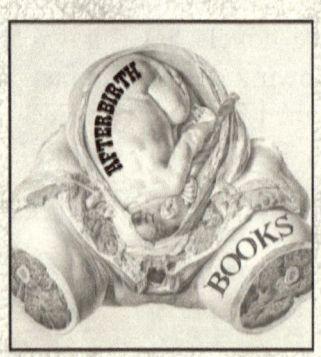

www.afterbirthbooks.com

www.swallowdownpress.com

For all your Bizarro needs visit:

WWW.BIZARROCENTRAL.COM

Introduce yourselves to the bizarro fiction genre and all of its authors with the Bizarro Starter Kit series. Each volume features short novels and short stories by ten of the leading bizarro authors, designed to give you a perfect sampling of the genre for only $10.

BB-0X1
"The Bizarro Starter Kit"
(Orange)
Featuring D. Harlan Wilson, Carlton Mellick III, Jeremy Robert Johnson, Kevin L Donihe, Gina Ranalli, Andre Duza, Vincent W. Sakowski, Steve Beard, John Edward Lawson, and Bruce Taylor. **236 pages $10**

BB-0X2
"The Bizarro Starter Kit"
(Blue)
Featuring Ray Fracalossy, Jeremy C. Shipp, Jordan Krall, Mykle Hansen, Andersen Prunty, Eckhard Gerdes, Bradley Sands, Steve Aylett, Christian TeBordo, and Tony Rauch. **244 pages $10**

BB-0X2
"The Bizarro Starter Kit"
(Purple)
Featuring Russell Edson, Athena Villaverde, David Agranoff, Matthew Revert, Andrew Goldfarb, Jeff Burk, Garrett Cook, Kris Saknussemm, Cody Goodfellow, and Cameron Pierce **264 pages $10**

BB-001"The Kafka Effekt" D. Harlan Wilson - A collection of forty-four irreal short stories loosely written in the vein of Franz Kafka, with more than a pinch of William S. Burroughs sprinkled on top. **211 pages $14**

BB-002 "Satan Burger" Carlton Mellick III - The cult novel that put Carlton Mellick III on the map ... Six punks get jobs at a fast food restaurant owned by the devil in a city violently overpopulated by surreal alien cultures. **236 pages $14**

BB-003 "Some Things Are Better Left Unplugged" Vincent Sakwoski - Join The Man and his Nemesis, the obese tabby, for a nightmare roller coaster ride into this postmodern fantasy. **152 pages $10**

BB-004 "Shall We Gather At the Garden?" Kevin L Donihe - Donihe's Debut novel. Midgets take over the world, The Church of Lionel Richie vs. The Church of the Byrds, plant porn and more! **244 pages $14**

BB-005 "Razor Wire Pubic Hair" Carlton Mellick III - A genderless humandildo is purchased by a razor dominatrix and brought into her nightmarish world of bizarre sex and mutilation.   **176 pages $11**

BB-006 "Stranger on the Loose" D. Harlan Wilson - The fiction of Wilson's 2nd collection is planted in the soil of normalcy, but what grows out of that soil is a dark, witty, otherworldly jungle... **228 pages $14**

BB-007 "The Baby Jesus Butt Plug" Carlton Mellick III - Using clones of the Baby Jesus for anal sex will be the hip sex fetish of the future. **92 pages $10**

BB-008 "Fishyfleshed" Carlton Mellick III - The world of the past is an illogical flatland lacking in dimension and color, a sick-scape of crispy squid people wandering the desert for no apparent reason. **260 pages $14**

BB-009 "Dead Bitch Army" Andre Duza - Step into a world filled with racist teenagers, cannibals, 100 warped Uncle Sams, automobiles with razor-sharp teeth, living graffiti, and a pissed-off zombie bitch out for revenge. **344 pages $16**

BB-010 "The Menstruating Mall" Carlton Mellick III - "The Breakfast Club meets Chopping Mall as directed by David Lynch." - Brian Keene **212 pages $12**

BB-011 "Angel Dust Apocalypse" Jeremy Robert Johnson - Meth-heads, man-made monsters, and murderous Neo-Nazis. "Seriously amazing short stories..." - Chuck Palahniuk, author of Fight Club **184 pages $11**

BB-012 "Ocean of Lard" Kevin L Donihe / Carlton Mellick III - A parody of those old Choose Your Own Adventure kid's books about some very odd pirates sailing on a sea made of animal fat. **176 pages $12**

BB-015 "Foop!" Chris Genoa - Strange happenings are going on at Dactyl, Inc, the world's first and only time travel tourism company.
"A surreal pie in the face!" - Christopher Moore **300 pages $14**

BB-020 "Punk Land" Carlton Mellick III - In the punk version of Heaven, the anarchist utopia is threatened by corporate fascism and only Goblin, Mortician's sperm, and a blue-mohawked female assassin named Shark Girl can stop them. **284 pages $15**

BB-021 "Pseudo-City" D. Harlan Wilson - Pseudo-City exposes what waits in the bathroom stall, under the manhole cover and in the corporate boardroom, all in a way that can only be described as mind-bogglingly irreal. **220 pages $16**

BB-023 "Sex and Death In Television Town" Carlton Mellick III - In the old west, a gang of hermaphrodite gunslingers take refuge from a demon plague in Telos: a town where its citizens have televisions instead of heads. **184 pages $12**

BB-027 "Siren Promised" Jeremy Robert Johnson & Alan M Clark
- Nominated for the Bram Stoker Award. A potent mix of bad drugs, bad dreams, brutal bad guys, and surreal/incredible art by Alan M. Clark. **190 pages $13**

BB-030 **"Grape City" Kevin L. Donihe** - More Donihe-style comedic bizarro about a demon named Charles who is forced to work a minimum wage job on Earth after Hell goes out of business. **108 pages $10**

BB-031 **"Sea of the Patchwork Cats" Carlton Mellick III** - A quiet dreamlike tale set in the ashes of the human race. For Mellick enthusiasts who also adore The Twilight Zone. **112 pages $10**

BB-032 **"Extinction Journals" Jeremy Robert Johnson** - An uncanny voyage across a newly nuclear America where one man must confront the problems associated with loneliness, insane dieties, radiation, love, and an ever-evolving cockroach suit with a mind of its own. **104 pages $10**

BB-034 **"The Greatest Fucking Moment in Sports" Kevin L. Donihe**
- In the tradition of the surreal anti-sitcom Get A Life comes a tale of triumph and agape love from the master of comedic bizarro. **108 pages $10**

BB-035 **"The Troublesome Amputee" John Edward Lawson** - Disturbing verse from a man who truly believes nothing is sacred and intends to prove it. **104 pages $9**

BB-037 **"The Haunted Vagina" Carlton Mellick III** - It's difficult to love a woman whose vagina is a gateway to the world of the dead. **132 pages $10**

BB-042 **"Teeth and Tongue Landscape" Carlton Mellick III** - On a planet made out of meat, a socially-obsessive monophobic man tries to find his place amongst the strange creatures and communities that he comes across. **110 pages $10**

BB-043 **"War Slut"** **Carlton Mellick III** - Part "1984," part "Waiting for Godot," and part action horror video game adaptation of John Carpenter's "The Thing." **116 pages $10**

BB-045 **"Dr. Identity"** **D. Harlan Wilson** - Follow the Dystopian Duo on a killing spree of epic proportions through the irreal postcapitalist city of Bliptown where time ticks sideways, artificial Bug-Eyed Monsters punish citizens for consumer-capitalist lethargy, and ultraviolence is as essential as a daily multivitamin. **208 pages $15**

BB-047 **"Sausagey Santa"** **Carlton Mellick III** - A bizarro Christmas tale featuring Santa as a piratey mutant with a body made of sausages. 124 pages $10

BB-048 **"Misadventures in a Thumbnail Universe"** **Vincent Sakowski** - Dive deep into the surreal and satirical realms of neo-classical Blender Fiction, filled with television shoes and flesh-filled skies. **120 pages $10**

BB-049 **"Vacation"** **Jeremy C. Shipp** - Blueblood Bernard Johnson leaved his boring life behind to go on The Vacation, a year-long corporate sponsored odyssey. But instead of seeing the world, Bernard is captured by terrorists, becomes a key figure in secret drug wars, and, worse, doesn't once miss his secure American Dream. **160 pages $14**

BB-053 **"Ballad of a Slow Poisoner"** **Andrew Goldfarb** Millford Mutterwurst sat down on a Tuesday to take his afternoon tea, and made the unpleasant discovery that his elbows were becoming flatter. **128 pages $10**

BB-055 **"Help! A Bear is Eating Me"** **Mykle Hansen** - The bizarro, heartwarming, magical tale of poor planning, hubris and severe blood loss...
150 pages $11

BB-056 **"Piecemeal June"** **Jordan Krall** - A man falls in love with a living sex doll, but with love comes danger when her creator comes after her with crab-squid assassins. **90 pages $9**

BB-058 "The Overwhelming Urge" Andersen Prunty - A collection of bizarro tales by Andersen Prunty. **150 pages $11**

BB-059 "Adolf in Wonderland" Carlton Mellick III - A dreamlike adventure that takes a young descendant of Adolf Hitler's design and sends him down the rabbit hole into a world of imperfection and disorder. **180 pages $11**

BB-061 "Ultra Fuckers" Carlton Mellick III - Absurdist suburban horror about a couple who enter an upper middle class gated community but can't find their way out. **108 pages $9**

BB-062 "House of Houses" Kevin L. Donihe - An odd man wants to marry his house. Unfortunately, all of the houses in the world collapse at the same time in the Great House Holocaust. Now he must travel to House Heaven to find his departed fiancee. **172 pages $11**

BB-064 "Squid Pulp Blues" Jordan Krall - In these three bizarro-noir novellas, the reader is thrown into a world of murderers, drugs made from squid parts, deformed gun-toting veterans, and a mischievous apocalyptic donkey. **204 pages $12**

BB-065 "Jack and Mr. Grin" Andersen Prunty - "When Mr. Grin calls you can hear a smile in his voice. Not a warm and friendly smile, but the kind that seizes your spine in fear. You don't need to pay your phone bill to hear it. That smile is in every line of Prunty's prose." - Tom Bradley. **208 pages $12**

BB-066 "Cybernetrix" Carlton Mellick III - What would you do if your normal everyday world was slowly mutating into the video game world from Tron? **212 pages $12**

BB-072 "Zerostrata" Andersen Prunty - Hansel Nothing lives in a tree house, suffers from memory loss, has a very eccentric family, and falls in love with a woman who runs naked through the woods every night. **144 pages $11**

BB-073 **"The Egg Man" Carlton Mellick III** - It is a world where humans reproduce like insects. Children are the property of corporations, and having an enormous ten-foot brain implanted into your skull is a grotesque sexual fetish. Mellick's industrial urban dystopia is one of his darkest and grittiest to date. **184 pages $11**

BB-074 **"Shark Hunting in Paradise Garden" Cameron Pierce** - A group of strange humanoid religious fanatics travel back in time to the Garden of Eden to discover it is invested with hundreds of giant flying maneating sharks. **150 pages $10**

BB-075 **"Apeshit" Carlton Mellick III** - Friday the 13th meets Visitor Q. Six hipster teens go to a cabin in the woods inhabited by a deformed killer. An incredibly fucked-up parody of B-horror movies with a bizarro slant. **192 pages $12**

BB-076 **"Fuckers of Everything on the Crazy Shitting Planet of the Vomit At smosphere" Mykle Hansen** - Three bizarro satires. Monster Cocks, Journey to the Center of Agnes Cuddlebottom, and Crazy Shitting Planet. **228 pages $12**

BB-077 **"The Kissing Bug" Daniel Scott Buck** - In the tradition of Roald Dahl, Tim Burton, and Edward Gorey, comes this bizarro anti-war children's story about a bohemian conenose kissing bug who falls in love with a human woman. **116 pages $10**

BB-078 **"MachoPoni" Lotus Rose** - It's My Little Pony... *Bizarro* style! A long time ago Poniworld was split in two. On one side of the Jagged Line is the Pastel Kingdom, a magical land of music, parties, and positivity. On the other side of the Jagged Line is Dark Kingdom inhabited by an army of undead ponies. **148 pages $11**

BB-079 **"The Faggiest Vampire" Carlton Mellick III** - A Roald Dahl-esque children's story about two faggy vampires who partake in a mustache competition to find out which one is truly the faggiest. **104 pages $10**

BB-080 **"Sky Tongues" Gina Ranalli** - The autobiography of Sky Tongues, the biracial hermaphrodite actress with tongues for fingers. Follow her strange life story as she rises from freak to fame. **204 pages $12**

BB-081 **"Washer Mouth" Kevin L. Donihe** - A washing machine becomes human and pursues his dream of meeting his favorite soap opera star. **244 pages $11**

BB-082 **"Shatnerquake" Jeff Burk** - All of the characters ever played by William Shatner are suddenly sucked into our world. Their mission: hunt down and destroy the real William Shatner. **100 pages $10**

BB-083 **"The Cannibals of Candyland" Carlton Mellick III** - There exists a race of cannibals that are made of candy. They live in an underground world made out of candy. One man has dedicated his life to killing them all. **170 pages $11**

BB-084 **"Slub Glub in the Weird World of the Weeping Willows"** **Andrew Goldfarb** - The charming tale of a blue glob named Slub Glub who helps the weeping willows whose tears are flooding the earth. There are also hyenas, ghosts, and a voodoo priest **100 pages $10**

BB-085 **"Super Fetus" Adam Pepper** - Try to abort this fetus and he'll kick your ass! **104 pages $10**

BB-086 **"Fistful of Feet" Jordan Krall** - A bizarro tribute to spaghetti westerns, featuring Cthulhu-worshipping Indians, a woman with four feet, a crazed gunman who is obsessed with sucking on candy, Syphilis-ridden mutants, sexually transmitted tattoos, and a house devoted to the freakiest fetishes. **228 pages $12**

BB-087 **"Ass Goblins of Auschwitz" Cameron Pierce** - It's Monty Python meets Nazi exploitation in a surreal nightmare as can only be imagined by Bizarro author Cameron Pierce. **104 pages $10**

BB-088 **"Silent Weapons for Quiet Wars" Cody Goodfellow** - "This is high-end psychological surrealist horror meets bottom-feeding low-life crime in a techno-thrilling science fiction world full of Lovecraft and magic..." -John Skipp **212 pages $12**

BB-089 "Warrior Wolf Women of the Wasteland" Carlton Mellick III
Road Warrior Werewolves versus McDonaldland Mutants...post-apocalyptic fiction has never been quite like this. **316 pages $13**

BB-090 "Cursed" Jeremy C Shipp - The story of a group of characters who believe they are cursed and attempt to figure out who cursed them and why. A tale of stylish absurdism and suspenseful horror. **218 pages $15**

BB-091 "Super Giant Monster Time" Jeff Burk - A tribute to choose your own adventures and Godzilla movies. Will you escape the giant monsters that are rampaging the fuck out of your city and shit? Or will you join the mob of alien-controlled punk rockers causing chaos in the streets? What happens next depends on you. **188 pages $12**

BB-092 "Perfect Union" Cody Goodfellow - "Cronenberg's THE FLY on a grand scale: human/insect gene-spliced body horror, where the human hive politics are as shocking as the gore." -John Skipp. **272 pages $13**

BB-093 "Sunset with a Beard" Carlton Mellick III - 14 stories of surreal science fiction. **200 pages $12**

BB-094 "My Fake War" Andersen Prunty - The absurd tale of an unlikely soldier forced to fight a war that, quite possibly, does not exist. It's Rambo meets Waiting for Godot in this subversive satire of American values and the scope of the human imagination. **128 pages $11**

BB-095"Lost in Cat Brain Land" Cameron Pierce - Sad stories from a surreal world. A fascist mustache, the ghost of Franz Kafka, a desert inside a dead cat. Primordial entities mourn the death of their child. The desperate serve tea to mysterious creatures.

A hopeless romantic falls in love with a pterodactyl. And much more. **152 pages $11**

BB-096 "The Kobold Wizard's Dildo of Enlightenment +2" Carlton Mellick III - A Dungeons and Dragons parody about a group of people who learn they are only made up characters in an AD&D campaign and must find a way to resist their nerdy teenaged players and retarded dungeon master in order to survive. **232 pages $12**

BB-097 **"My Heart Said No, but the Camera Crew Said Yes!" Bradley Sands** - A collection of short stories that are crammed with the delightfully odd and the scurrilously silly. **140 pages $13**

BB-098 **"A Hundred Horrible Sorrows of Ogner Stump" Andrew Goldfarb** - Goldfarb's acclaimed comic series. A magical and weird journey into the horrors of everyday life. **164 pages $11**

BB-099 **"Pickled Apocalypse of Pancake Island" Cameron Pierce** A demented fairy tale about a pickle, a pancake, and the apocalypse. **102 pages $8**

BB-100 **"Slag Attack" Andersen Prunty** - Slag Attack features four visceral, noir stories about the living, crawling apocalypse.A slag is what survivors are calling the slug-like maggots raining from the sky, burrowing inside people, and hollowing out their flesh and their sanity. **148 pages $11**

BB-101 **"Slaughterhouse High" Robert Devereaux** - A place where schools are built with secret passageways, rebellious teens get zippers installed in their mouths and genitals, and once a year, on that special night, one couple is slaughtered and the bits of their bodies are kept as souvenirs. **304 pages $13**

BB-102 **"The Emerald Burrito of Oz" John Skipp & Marc Levinthal** OZ IS REAL! Magic is real! The gate is really in Kansas! And America is finally allowing Earth tourists to visit this weird-ass, mysterious land. But when Gene of Los Angeles heads off for summer vacation in the Emerald City, little does he know that a war is brewing...a war that could destroy both worlds. **280 pages $13**

BB-103 **"The Vegan Revolution... with Zombies" David Agranoff** When there's no more meat in hell, the vegans will walk the earth. **160 pages $11**

BB-104 **"The Flappy Parts" Kevin L Donihe** - Poems about bunnies, LSD, and police abuse. You know, things that matter. 132 **pages $11**

BB-105 "Sorry I Ruined Your Orgy" Bradley Sands - Bizarro humorist
Bradley Sands returns with one of the strangest, most hilarious collections of the year.
130 pages $11

BB-106 "Mr. Magic Realism" Bruce Taylor - Like Golden Age science fiction comics written by Freud, *Mr. Magic Realism* is a strange, insightful adventure that spans the furthest reaches of the galaxy, exploring the hidden caverns in the hearts and minds of men, women, aliens, and biomechanical cats. 152 pages $11

BB-107 "Zombies and Shit" Carlton Mellick III - "Battle Royale" meets "Return of the Living Dead." Mellick's bizarro tribute to the zombie genre. 308 pages $13

BB-108 "The Cannibal's Guide to Ethical Living" Mykle Hansen - Over a five star French meal of fine wine, organic vegetables and human flesh, a lunatic delivers a witty, chilling, disturbingly sane argument in favor of eating the rich.. 184 pages $11

BB-109 "Starfish Girl" Athena Villaverde - In a post-apocalyptic underwater dome society, a girl with a starfish growing from her head and an assassin with sea anenome hair are on the run from a gang of mutant fish men. 160 pages $11

BB-110 "Lick Your Neighbor" Chris Genoa - Mutant ninjas, a talking whale, kung fu masters, maniacal pilgrims, and an alcoholic clown populate Chris Genoa's surreal, darkly comical and unnerving reimagining of the first Thanksgiving. 303 pages $13

BB-111 "Night of the Assholes" Kevin L. Donihe - A plague of assholes is infecting the countryside. Normal everyday people are transforming into jerks, snobs, dicks, and douchebags. And they all have only one purpose: to make your life a living hell.. 192 pages $11

BB-112 "Jimmy Plush, Teddy Bear Detective" Garrett Cook - Hardboiled cases of a private detective trapped within a teddy bear body. 180 pages $11

www.ingramcontent.com/pod-product-compliance
Lightning Source LLC
Chambersburg PA
CBHW020731250626
47155CB00006B/2247